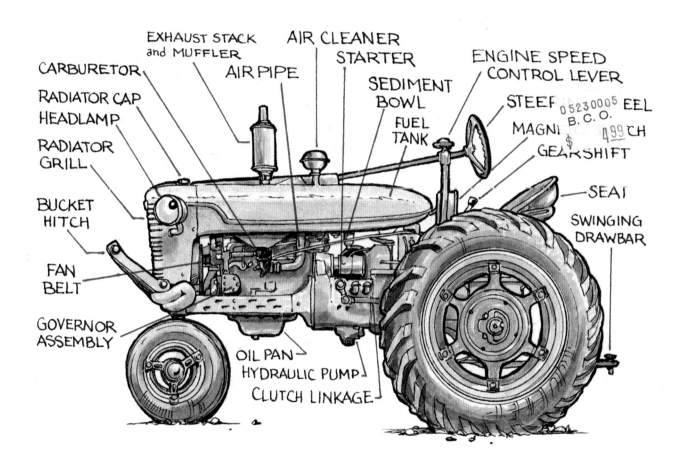

CARBURETOR

RADIATOR CAP
HEADLAMP

RADIATOR
GRILL

BUCKET
HITCH

FAN
BELT

GOVERNOR
ASSEMBLY

EXHAUST STACK
and MUFFLER
AIR PIPE

AIR CLEANER
STARTER

SEDIMENT
BOWL
FUEL
TANK

ENGINE SPEED
CONTROL LEVER

STEER 05230005 EEL
B.C.O.
MAGN $ 499 CH
GEARSHIFT

SEAT

SWINGING
DRAWBAR

OIL PAN
HYDRAULIC PUMP
CLUTCH LINKAGE

Tractor Mac

This book is for Julie.
Love, Billy

Text © 1999 by Billy Steers. Illustrations © 1999 by Billy Steers. All rights reserved. Printed in Italy. No part of this book may be reproduced or copied in any form without written permission from the publisher. GOLDEN BOOKS®, A GOLDEN BOOK®, GOLDEN BOOKS FAMILY STORYTIME™, and G DESIGN™ are trademarks of Golden Books Publishing Company, Inc. Library of Congress Catalog Card number: 98-87172 ISBN: 0-307-10224-6   A MCMXCIX

This book has a reinforced trade binding.

TRACTOR MAC

written and illustrated by **Billy Steers**

A Golden Book • New York
Golden Books Publishing Company, Inc.
New York, New York 10106

Sibley the horse lived on Stony Meadow Farm.
He was a hard worker. Tug and pull, haul and drag.
He did the work of two strong horses.

Sibley's days were spent plowing in the spring,

mowing in the summer,

harvesting in the fall,

and logging in the winter.

Sibley's favorite job was pulling the hayride at the summer picnics.

The children would all cheer for Sibley and give him treats of apples and carrots.

One day, the animals heard a strange new noise
in the farmyard. *Chug! Chugga! Pop!*
They looked out of the barn.

A large red machine sat in the farmyard spewing
smoke. Farmer Bill was seated on a bright, new
shiny tractor. He had a big smile on his face.

That evening Farmer Bill parked the tractor in the barn. The animals came over to greet the newcomer.

"What big, black rubber tires you have," said Carla the Chicken.

"Look at all of your wires, gears, and cables!"
exclaimed Pete the Pig.

"Welcome to Stony Meadow Farm," greeted
Sam the old ram.

"Welcome! Welcome!" the others cried.

The red tractor smiled. "Howdy Do!" he said.
"My name is Mac. I can do the work of ten
horses and I'm happy to be here."

"Ten horses!" gasped the animals. "You must be
really strong."

That night, Sibley was not able to sleep. Visions of mechanical horses danced in his head. Could Mac really do the work of ten horses? What would be left for Sibley to do?

Early the next morning, Farmer Bill climbed into Mac's seat and started the engine. Mac rumbled to life, and they headed for the fields.

Sibley waited to be tacked up for the day's work, but nobody came.

All day, Sibley listened to the other animals.

"Did you see how fast Mac plowed the fields?" cackled the chickens.

"He delivered the hay in less than an hour," the sheep exclaimed.

"He hauled all the wood for the new roof," squealed the pigs.

As the days passed, it was clear that Mac had taken over all of Sibley's jobs.

"Soon they'll be turning you out to pasture," said Margot the cow. "You'll probably never have to work another day in your life."

Just then, Sibley heard the sound of children.
Maybe they were coming to the barnyard for a
hayride. He galloped out of the barn. . . .

. . . and stopped abruptly at the fence. There was
Mac, pulling a dozen cheering children in a hay
wagon. Sibley's hay wagon!

Sibley had never felt so sad and useless in his whole life. What good is a workhorse who cannot work?

In the weeks that followed, Sibley hoped he
would be put to work. But every morning, Farmer
Bill and Mac left the barn. Sibley wondered if he
had been forgotten for good.

Finally, one day, Farmer Bill came back to the farm without Mac. "Sibley, old lad, I need your help. We have a problem that only you can fix."

The farmer led Sibley to one of the far fields. Rain had fallen during the night. The field was soaked with rainwater. There sat Mac up to his axles in mud.

With a tug and a yank, Sibley wrenched the tractor free from the mud.

Then he spent the rest of the day working in the soggy field while Mac sat behind the stone wall.

When it was time to go back to the barn,
Mac said, "Thanks for rescuing me, Sibley."
Farmer Bill patted Sibley on the neck.
"You were a big help today," he said.

From that day on, Farmer Bill let both Sibley
and Mac work side by side. They became the best
of friends.

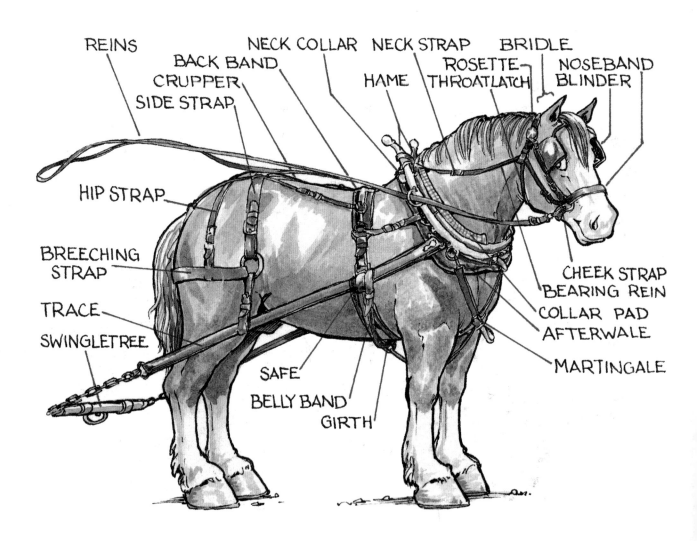

REINS

BACK BAND
NECK COLLAR   NECK STRAP   BRIDLE
CRUPPER   ROSETTE   NOSEBAND
SIDE STRAP   HAME   THROATLATCH   BLINDER

HIP STRAP

BREECHING
STRAP

TRACE

SWINGLETREE

CHEEK STRAP
BEARING REIN
COLLAR PAD
AFTERWALE

MARTINGALE

SAFE
BELLY BAND
GIRTH

Sibley